"Dear friends, let us love one another,

for love comes from God."

1 John 4:7

ZONDERKIDZ

The Berenstain Bears: The Trouble with Secrets

Copyright © 1992, 2011 by Berenstain Publishing, Inc.
Illustrations © 1992, 2011 by Berenstain Publishing, Inc.

Requests for information should be addressed to:
Zonderkidz, Grand Rapids, Michigan 49530

Library of Congress Cataloging-in-Publication Data

Berenstain, Jan, 1923–
      The Berenstain Bears: the trouble with secrets / Jan Berenstain and Mike
Berenstain.
            p. cm.
            ISBN 978-0-310-72713-2 (hardback)
         [1. Stories in rhyme. 2. Secrets—Fiction. 3. Friendship—Fiction. 4. Christian life—
Fiction. 5. Bears—Fiction. 6. Animals—Fiction.] I. Berenstain, Mike, 1951- II. Title. III.
Title: Trouble with secrets.
      PZ8.3.B44925Be   2011
      [E]—dc22   2010052436

Editor: Mary Hassinger
Art direction: Diane Mielke

Printed in China

---

11 12 13 14 15 16 /SCC/ 10 9 8 7 6 5 4 3 2 1

The Berenstain Bears®
The Trouble
with Secrets

by Stan and Jan Berenstain
with Mike Berenstain

 ZONDERVAN.com/
AUTHORTRACKER
follow your favorite authors

 ZONDER**kidz**

 Living
Lights™

There go Brother and Sister Bear.
Friends Lizzy and Fred
want to know where.

Lizzy and Fred want to know why
their friends have that
secret look in their eye.

Is this something our friends would do?
Keep a secret from me and you?

Where are our friends going today?
We know what!
We'll ask Mr. Jay!

But he just says, "Screech!"
He will not say
where Brother and Sister
are going today.

He must have promised
he would not say!

SCREECH

So we follow our friends
to where the path bends.

We follow and follow
and follow along.
We hear Mrs. Cricket singing her song
of how thankful she is
that God's love is so strong.

We ask Mrs. Cricket
if she will say
where Brother and Sister
are going today.

But she just chirps.
She will not say.
She will not give the secret away.
She must have promised
she would not say!

We make sure we are not seen
as we move through the forest
so dark and so green.

We follow and follow
and follow along.
Friends Brother and Sister
are still going strong.

Should we ask Mr. Skunk?
He might know
where Brother and Sister
are about to go.

Hmmm. On second thought ...
we don't think we ought!

We follow our friends
through Great Grizzly Bog,
where Mrs. Frog suns herself
on Great Hollow Log ...

and ribbits a prayer
of thanks and praise
for flies and water and hot, sunny days.

Should we ask Mrs. Frog?
It's worth a try.

But she sticks out her tongue
and catches a fly.
Yuck! We think it's time to say good-bye.

So we follow and follow
and follow along.

Friends Brother and Sister
are still going strong.

Now we see
old Mr. Croc

sound asleep
on a big rock.

We do not bother
old Mr. Croc.
We leave him sleeping
on his rock.

We're getting tired following along
and following and following
and following along.
There is no need for secrets or sneaking.
God made us friends!
If they'd share, we'd stop peeking!

Will this following
NEVER END?

But wait! Brother and Sister
are rounding a bend!

And look at that! Standing right there!
The secret of Brother
and Sister Bear!
It's a clubhouse they made
from pieces of junk.

"Who told?" asked Brother.
"Was it Mr. Skunk?
Or Frog or Croc or Cricket or Jay
who told you our secret
and showed you the way?"

"Nobody told.
Though you were really going strong,
we just followed and followed
and followed along!"
Brother and Sister looked glum for a while.
But being upset
just isn't their style!
Then they both began to smile.

They were glad God blessed them
with friends like Lizzy and Fred.
"We're glad you followed us here," they said.

"Secrets are fun.
But it's more fun to share!
So welcome!" said Brother
and Sister Bear.